The Vintage Tea Room

*end of an era and
new beginnings*

Lily Wells

1

Ellie did a final check of the tea room – fresh flowers, clean tablecloths and straight pictures. From the moment she'd bought this place she knew she'd wanted to create a traditional tea room. Vintage but not old fashioned. In an age of wipe clean tables and large mugs she'd gone for tablecloths covered with English flowers, white napkins, cups with saucers, and patterned wallpaper.

She'd arranged for the photographer to come on a Tuesday because she usually had a little more time during the morning, it was still busy but as she did a lot of preparation for the week on a Monday she could almost relax.

She loved this time of day especially when, like today, the morning sun streamed through the windows. Even though the street outside was narrow with shops on both sides it never appeared dark or dingy, the sunlight found its way through and added a brightness to the honey coloured Cotswold stone buildings. With the tables and chairs outside she thought this area almost had a Parisian feel. Ellie took a moment to watch people as they wandered down the street, some on their way to work, others out shopping, and a few tourists looking through their guide books and taking photos as they admired the historic buildings.

Ellie took one last glance before turning back to the job in hand, soon this view would no longer be hers. She turned on the coffee machine behind the counter before going into the adjoining kitchen to turn on the urn. As she collected the cakes from the fridge the bell on the tea room door jingled.

"Hi, is that you Joe," she called out without looking round.

"Who's Joe?" came the reply.

"Jessica, what are you doing here?" Ellie said as she hurried back into the tea room.

"Good to see you too, Mum," Jessica said, "and again, who is Joe?"

"Joe's the photographer, but never mind that, is everything okay?" Ellie said looking at Jessica's tiny bump. She'd been over the moon when she'd heard Jessica was expecting her first baby.

"I'm fine, or rather the baby's fine, I've left Edward and come back here to live," Jessica said as she sat at one of the tables and put her bag on the floor.

"Oh, Jessie," said Ellie putting her arm around her shoulders. "What's happened?"

Before Jessica could answer the doorbell jingled again.

"Hi, Ellie," said a young man with a camera around his neck. "Is now a good time?" he asked looking from Ellie to Jessica. "The office said to come early before you had customers."

"Now's perfect," said Ellie smiling.

Ellie turned back to Jessica. "Give me ten minutes to show Joe around and then I'll make some tea and you can tell me everything."

"Fine," replied Jessica. "I'll take my things up to my room."

"Actually, could you wait in the back room," said Ellie looking a little sheepishly at Jessica. "Joe needs to take some photos upstairs."

Ellie caught the look of annoyance of Jessica's face as she got up and went through to the hallway.

"Sorry about that," Ellie said looking back at Joe. "Unexpected visit."

"No worries," Joe said. "Show me around and then I'll start snapping. I'll start outside since the sun's out. I must say this place has real appeal, I think you'll get a buyer in no time."

"I hope so," said Ellie, "now I've made the decision to

2

sell I'd like to get things moving quickly."

"I think we have a number of people on our books looking for a home and business. They're mostly families hoping to find that dream lifestyle. And, let's face it, you don't get much better than this - Cotswold location, vibrant town, something for all the family, it's the perfect package," said Joe smiling.

"Wow, how could anyone resist," Ellie said laughing.

"I should be able to get some really good shots so lead the way," Joe said.

Ellie led Joe into the kitchen and on through to the office behind. She then doubled back and took him into the hallway that led to the main house which was mainly above the tea room.

To the right of the stairs was a small sitting room, affectionately called the back room, with French doors leading out onto the courtyard. Ellie looked at the closed door, she hoped Jessica would be alright for a few minutes.

"You'd best do this room last," Ellie said. "I need to explain to Jessica first."

Joe followed Ellie upstairs where she gave him a whistle-stop tour of the rooms - kitchen, sitting room, bathroom and four bedrooms. She'd spent the last two weeks sprucing it up a little ready to sell. She'd painted, bought new bed linen and some new rugs. And, of course, did the obligatory de-clutter.

"I'll leave you to it," Ellie said. "You've got about an hour until we open."

"That's plenty of time," Joe said. "I'll find you when I'm done."

2

Ellie went back down to the kitchen and put the kettle on; the water in the urn wasn't yet hot enough to use. She loved the routine of preparing a pot of tea - warming the pot, laying a tray and putting milk, lemon and sugar into the little containers. Twenty-three years ago she might have thought this was a lot of fuss for one cup of tea, now she knew better.

She selected a Breakfast Tea, a perfect pick-me-up in the morning. Ellie put the pot on the tray and carried it through to the back room. Calling this the back room didn't do it justice, it was a pretty, bright room that had served many purposes. Years ago it had been the playroom for the twins and then a room for them to bring their friends when they wanted to be cool and not be too close to their mother. Now it had a sofa, a small wicker and glass dining set and her CD player. She would often sit here when she took a break from work or during the evening, especially in the summer when she opened up the French doors and allowed the warm air to drift into the room.

Jessica was sitting at the table looking out into the courtyard. Ellie followed her gaze towards the large pots of daffodils just outside the doors. Daffodils were one of her favourite flowers, they heralded in the warmer weather even if they often appeared when it was snowing, raining or bitterly cold, and they had that magical ability to make her smile.

"Here you go, Jessica," Ellie said as she put the tray on the table and poured two cups of tea. "Now tell me what's happened."

"I think you'd better tell me what's going on with Joe. Are you being photographed for one of those lifestyle magazines?" asked Jessica.

"Not exactly, I'll explain later. You go first, have you

had a row?" asked Ellie.

Jessica let out a sob. "No, I just can't live with him anymore, he's...," she paused, "he's suffocating me," she said.

"What do you mean, I thought you two were great together, I'd never had him down as the possessive type," Ellie said. Edward had always seemed a great guy, reliable, wouldn't do anything to hurt Jessica.

"He's not, it's just that since I got pregnant things have changed," Jessica said.

"How?" asked Ellie.

"Well, every weekend he wants to paint the nursery or look at prams or talk about baby names," Jessica said.

"That doesn't sound too bad," Ellie said, smiling.

"You wouldn't understand," Jessica said.

Ellie could see tears form in the corner of her eyes.

"Try me," Ellie said.

"We used to go out, meet friends, have fun," Jessica said, the tears had started to fall down her cheeks.

"I thought you were pleased about the baby, and it sounds like Edward is really happy too, so what's wrong?" said Ellie.

"I am pleased, but we don't have to spend every spare minute preparing," said Jessica, sobbing.

"Getting ready for the baby is important, but you're right, you do need time to adjust as things will be very different once the baby's born. Maybe it's Edward's way of getting involved, you know, doing his bit to help," said Ellie. She put an arm around her daughter.

"I know I sound selfish, but the baby doesn't have to become our entire focus," said Jessica.

"Trust me, he or she will take up most of your waking hours, at least for the first few months. Have you told Edward how you feel?" Ellie asked.

"No, he'll only tell me that feeling like this is normal and I'll soon get excited about the whole thing," Jessica said. She took a tissue from her bag and wiped her eyes. The tears had stopped and she began to sound a little bit calmer.

"Maybe he's wiser than you think," said Ellie.

"Don't you start, I came here for a bit of support," Jessica said.

"You have told him you're here?" Ellie asked.

"Not yet," Jessica replied looking into her cup.

"You know you're welcome to stay for as long as you like but you do need to tell him where you are, it's not fair to let him worry," Ellie said.

"I'll text him later, he'll be busy now," Jessica said. "And he won't know I'm gone until he gets home tonight."

"Don't you think he deserves a phone call," Ellie said gently, trying to avoid upsetting Jessica again.

"I guess, but I don't want to hear him fussing," Jessica said.

Ellie sipped her tea and stared at the little roses around the top of the cup. When she'd first arrived in Cirencester the only thing she knew about tea was how to put a teabag into a mug and yet she'd decided tea was going to be her speciality and the little café she had bought was going to be a proper tea room. She'd read books, visited tea merchants, attended fairs, tasted samples and even visited a plantation in Africa. Eventually she felt she had a pretty reasonable knowledge of the different teas and blends. Her customers could choose from a good selection from across the world and, if needed, she could offer them advice. Despite the growing trend for coffee shops, several had opened in the town and were very popular, her tea room had kept its customers and attracted the tourists. During the summer it was usually full and even in winter she was kept busy.

"Your turn mum," Jessica said breaking into her thoughts. "What's going on with Joe?"

"He's from the estate agent, he's taking the photos for the brochure," Ellie replied.

"What brochure?" Jessica asked putting her cup down and looking directly at Ellie.

Ellie looked at Jessica, she hadn't planned to tell her like this but, as she couldn't avoid it, she might as well just say it.

"I'm selling the tea room," said Ellie.

"Selling, you can't sell, this is our home. When were you going to discuss this with us, or have you already spoken to Marie, I bet you have, you always tell her everything first just because she's the oldest," Jessica said rushing the words out.

"You're twins born minutes apart so I don't think that counts as older. I was going to tell you both before it goes on the market, probably next week," said Ellie.

"But you can't sell our home," Jessica said.

"It's too big for me and I want to do something different," said Ellie.

"Like what? You're too young to retire," said Jessica.

"I'm not retiring, I just thought I'd try a change of direction that's all," Ellie said, she was a little surprised at Jessica's reaction after all she hadn't lived here for quite some years now and rarely stayed overnight when she did visit.

Joe popped his head into the back room.

"Nearly done," he said. "I'll get some photos of the courtyard then I'll be finished. We'll get the brochure put together and I'll bring a copy across."

"Thanks, go on through," Ellie said.

"You can't really be selling, what will you do?" said Jessica when Joe was out of earshot.

"I'm downsizing, I think that's the fashionable term. I'm going to keep the cake side of the business and run that from the cottage. And I intend to travel, you know all the places I've dreamed of visiting. I'll also be able to see more of you and your sister, as you know it's always been difficult to get away," Ellie said.

"Back up a bit. What cottage?" asked Jessica.

"The one I'm going to buy," said Ellie realising that perhaps she should have told the girls beforehand but, to be honest, she didn't think they'd be that interested. After all they were leading their own lives now.

"This all seems a bit sudden, don't you think you should take some time to think it through properly?" said Jessica.

"It's not that sudden. I saw the cottage a month or so ago, that's what made me decide to sell. Bit of fate really, I was driving to deliver a cake just outside Cirencester and passed this lovely cottage with a for sale sign. As luck would have it the owner was outside and we had a chat. She kindly showed me around and, well the place was perfect so I put in an offer and decided to sell," said Ellie.

"But Mum, this is our family home," Jessica said with a hint of pleading in her voice.

"Both you and your sister moved out a long time ago, it hasn't been a family home for some while. It's time it had a new lease of life. Come on I'll help you with your things, your room's pretty much the same but I have given it a lick of paint. And some of your bits are stored under the bed. A bit of staging can only help the sale," she said laughing.

Jessica looked at her scowling. "I don't think this is anything to laugh about," she said.

Joe came back in from the courtyard so Ellie decided not to respond. Maybe Jessica just needed some time to get used to the idea.

3

Ellie left Jessica resting in her bedroom, the early morning start and train journey from Bristol had left her looking tired. Add to that the shock of learning she was selling the tea room, even though she had been surprised at her reaction, and she probably needed to catch up on her sleep. She had initially been surprised that Jessica hadn't driven up but she'd soon realised that coming here was a bit of a sudden decision and her husband, Edward, had the car. Ellie would need to make sure Jessica got in touch with him, from what Jessica had said he clearly cared about her and didn't even realise Jessica was unhappy.

Ellie went back into the kitchen and put on her apron ready to open up. With the glorious spring weather and less than a week to go before the school holidays the early tourists would be out in force. Pat would be here shortly, it was just the two of them this week as the seasonal staff didn't start until next Monday, just before the Easter weekend.

Pat had been a real godsend when she'd first opened the tea room. Not only did she know how to make a proper pot of tea she also made the most exquisite miniature cakes. The customers loved them, instead of having to choose one large slice of cake, always difficult when they all looked so good, they could select three or four miniatures and try them all. It was when Ellie had first displayed these miniatures on a tiered cake stand that she'd had the idea to offer proper afternoon tea with delicate looking cakes and sandwiches rather than a full lunch menu.

The bell on the door jingled again as Pat came into the tea room. As usual she was dressed in her black trousers and white top. Even though Ellie hadn't initially had a uniform for staff, she'd only insisted on them wearing a white apron, Pat's black and white dress code was adopted by herself and soon became the dress code for all her staff.

"Morning Ellie," said Pat. "Has the photographer been."

"Yes," said Ellie, it was a good job Jessica was still upstairs, she'd be really annoyed that Pat knew about the sale. "He says he's got some great shots."

"I'm going to miss you," said Pat as she put on her apron.

"I won't be that far away, and I'll probably pop back in for a quick cuppa," said Ellie.

"I'm not sure I'll be here," said Pat.

"The new owners are bound to want you to stay," Ellie said, "you know this place inside out."

"Maybe, but I'm sure they'll want to put their own stamp on the place and, as you know, I've never been that good with change," Pat said. "I have been thinking about retiring."

"The regulars will miss you. I think some of them come in more for a chat with you than a cup of tea," Ellie said laughing.

With that the first customer of the day arrived. Margaret came in every Tuesday and Thursday, usually as soon as they opened. She lived in one of the villages outside the town and caught the bus in to do her shopping and visit her sister. Ellie always admired the effort Margaret took with her appearance, her grey hair was pinned up, make-up was carefully applied and her clothes were well put together. Ellie had never made that much effort to go shopping.

"Morning Margaret," said Ellie, "your usual?"

"Yes please," said Margaret as she sat at a table next to the window.

Ellie made a pot of Earl Grey tea, laid a tray and carried it across to Margaret.

"The cake's on me," she said indicating a miniature slice of lemon sponge topped with a lemon glaze. "A new recipe, let me know what you think."

"Thank you," said Margaret as she poured the tea into her cup. "If it tastes as good as it looks it'll be a sure fire winner."

Ellie genuinely valued the opinion of her customers, especially those who came back week after week and kept her in business during the winter. She trusted their comments and if several customers said they didn't think a cake was right for the tea room then she'd take their advice. Some customers even brought in their own recipes for her to try, the idea had become so popular that she now had a customer special cake every month. Margaret herself had contributed a recipe for a fruit cake using dried fruit soaked in tea – everyone had loved it and there had been several requests for the recipe.

Within an hour the tea room was buzzing, most of the tables were taken, many with people who were visiting the area. Several asked Ellie which were the best places to visit. She usually named a few she'd visited herself such as the Corinium Museum and the Arboretum. She always suggested they visit a few of the shops in the older buildings with their maze of rooms and uneven floors as this was interesting for the visitors and usually good business for the local stores. If the weather was good she'd also recommend taking a walk in the Abbey Grounds to see a little of the town's Roman history.

As was usual in the morning Pat made up a selection of sandwiches and, if they were needed, baked some cakes before giving Ellie a hand with serving the customers. Ellie could already smell the delicious aroma of warm cakes. As she headed back towards the kitchen with an order for sandwiches another customer walked through the door, a man wearing a navy suit, white shirt and one of those picture ties that were using bought by children for their father – this one was covered with rabbits. He looked like he was popping in during a break from work. Occasionally people walked in wanting a coffee to go, this was one of the things she had decided not to offer. She wanted people to take the time to enjoy their tea, or coffee, and she liked to have a little time, even if only a few minutes, to chat with her customers.

Ellie looked at the man and smiled. "Can I help?" she said. "Would you like a table?"

"No, thanks," he said. "I wanted to order a birthday cake, your sign in the window says you make any design to order."

"We do," Ellie said looking around the busy room, she always wanted to make all of her customers feel welcome but now was not a great time to discuss cake designs.

"Take a seat," Ellie said gesturing to an empty table. "I'll just be a minute."

She asked Pat to take over in the tea room and grabbed her file of photos she'd taken of the cakes she'd made and a few ideas for themes.

"I'm Ellie, I may need to keep popping up to serve, unless you'd prefer to come back later when it's a bit quieter," said Ellie as she sat opposite him.

"I'm Michael," said the man. "I realise you're busy but I'd like to order now if that's possible. I looking to buy a cake for a birthday party and a want something a bit special, well very special actually."

"I make to order so I can do pretty much any theme you want, when's the party?" asked Ellie.

"This weekend," said Michael.

Ellie looked up in surprise. "This weekend, as in five days away? You're cutting it fine. I can certainly do something but I usually work to a three week turnaround to allow enough time to plan the design and create the decorations," she said.

"Sorry," Michael said, "it was a bit of a last minute decision. Grace has been unwell for quite a while and has been in and out of hospital for the last few months. She's well enough for a party now, her birthday was actually six weeks ago but she was in hospital. I wanted something really special, something that would do a bit more than make her smile.

"Of course I'll do my best," Ellie said, smiling. "How old is Grace?"

"Nine," Michael replied.

Ellie smiled at him. "Let's have a look at some examples and see if there's anything you like," she said.

She opened the file and showed Michael some of the photos of the cakes she'd made in the past.

"This one was for a little boy, he was mad about spiders so I made this cake like a giant spider on a web. I had to make the spider look friendly as I didn't want to scare the other children," she said. "I'm guessing not what you want for a little girl."

She flicked through to another that was made up of individual cupcakes each decorated slightly differently and with a name iced onto each. "This one was for a wedding anniversary, they wanted it to show how important each one of their friends and family were to them," she said. "These probably aren't what you are looking for but there are some themes here around Halloween, football, and horse-riding."

She continued to turn the pages but even though Michael made positive comments his face didn't seem to light up to any of them. Ellie closed the file.

"Perhaps the cupcake idea would be nice," he said.

Ellie looked at him and smiled. "I can design something specifically for Grace, perhaps a favourite hobby, but we'll have to be quick as I'll need to start tonight. What does Grace like most of all?" Ellie asked.

Michael looked thoughtful for a moment. "She likes fairies, could you do something that includes them. I'm sorry, I'm not great when it comes to imagination," he said.

"I'll give it some thought tonight, can you come back tomorrow morning and I'll run some ideas by you," Ellie said. "In the meantime I'll need to get on with baking the cake, how many people is it for and what type of cake do you want – sponge, fruit, chocolate?"

"Wow, all these choices," Michael said laughing. "There'll be about twelve children and a quite a few family so maybe enough for thirty. Sponge I guess, could it be purple, it's her favourite colour?"

"Purple sponge it is," Ellie said as she stood up. "Pop in tomorrow before ten, I'm sure I can come up with something she'll like."

Ellie watched Michael leave, she had no idea who Grace was, however, clearly this birthday party was important and Michael wanted it to be perfect. All she had to do was deliver a cake in just four and a half days.

As Ellie cleared a few tables Jessica walked into the tea room.

"Come to help?" asked Ellie.

Jessica laughed. "I know you're busy so I've arranged to see some old friends. I'll be back this evening and then we can talk properly. Maybe talk about the future - yours and mine," she said.

Ellie watched as she left. She felt the urge to go after her and tell her they could talk now. With that two more customers came in. She couldn't leave Pat on her own so it would have to wait.

4

Jessica hadn't returned by the time Ellie closed the tea room, she wasn't too surprised as Jessica had said she'd be back later that evening. Although something was obviously troubling her she didn't seem too distressed. Whatever it was she hoped she'd share it soon. She popped a chicken casserole in the oven, if Jessica wasn't hungry she could warm it up another day.

Now seemed a good time to start on the cake for Michael, if she was going to get it finished she needed to get a move on. Ellie did most of her baking in the tea room kitchen, there were some practical reasons such as two good ovens and a pantry full of ingredients however the main reason she like being downstairs was because she could look through the window and watch the evening walkers and night-time revellers walking past. There was a predictability about people at different times of the night, early evening a few people were walking dogs or popping to get milk, a little later people were dressed up to meet friends and enjoy a meal or drink, occasionally there might be couples walking together, and later everyone made their way back home – often rather noisily. This gave her a sense of time moving on rather than standing still as it had done when she'd first had the news that James had been killed. In the early years she could put the twins to bed and come down here, she always took the baby monitor with her, even when they got older, just to be sure they were safe.

Before she'd baked she'd had this vast stretch of time, night after night, to think of the past and the injustice of it all. Her grief had started to crush her. A chance conversation with a customer led her to making first one, and then many, celebration cakes. With her waking hours filled she had been able to start to rebuild a life for her and the twins.

Ellie took the scales from the shelf, weighed out the flour and sieved it into the mixing bowl. She then added the sugar, butter and eggs. Finally, she combined the ingredients in her mixer setting it at a slow speed to start before turning it up to get a nice fluffy texture. The large red mixer had been a present to herself, she'd seen it in a cook shop in the town and bought it on impulse. It always made her smile when she used it, it made her feel like a proper cook.

Once the mixture had a light and fluffy look she divided it between two bowls and added some pink colouring to one bowl and purple to the other. She then carefully folded the two mixtures together to get a marbled effect.

Ellie divided the mixture between three tins, two would make up a tiered cake and the last would be used to cut out some additional shapes if needed. She kept a little mixture back to make some cupcakes for Michael to try tomorrow.

As she put the cakes into the oven and set the timer Jessica walked into the kitchen.

"Can I help?" Jessica asked.

"Since when have you been interested in baking?" Ellie said laughing.

"Well, I could learn," Jessica replied.

"I've pretty much finished tonight but you can help tidy up," Ellie said.

"Washing up, that brings back memories," Jessica said collecting the bowls from the worktop.

"Don't worry, I've invested in a dishwasher, the mixer will have to be washed by hand though," Ellie said as she filled the sink with warm water.

Jessica sat down on a stool. "You know I've always loved this place, it holds so many memories, good memories," she said.

Ellie smiled at her, she was about to ask her why she

was here when there was a knock on the door.

Ellie looked across the tea room and could see a familiar face pressed against the door. It was Edward, Jessica's husband.

"Hi," she said after she'd unlocked the door and let Edward in.

Edward rushed across the room. "Jessica, what's the matter?" he said. "I got your text and came as soon as I could, is everything alright?"

"Oh Jessica," Ellie said. "I thought you were going to ring him."

"I was," she replied looking annoyed, "tonight."

Ellie went back to the kitchen to clear up and put the cakes on a cooling tray but she couldn't help but overhear their conversation.

"I just want some time on my own," Jessica said. "I had to get away."

"Are you feeling okay?" Edward asked with genuine concern in his voice.

"Yes, I'm fine, in fact I've never felt better," Jessica said.

"I guess a rest would be good for you at the moment," he said.

"I don't need a rest, I need a normal life," Jessica said.

"I get the feeling something's wrong but I've no idea what it is, tell me and then we can sort it out," Edward said.

Ellie watched Jessica take a deep breath, she looked as if she was about to scream at Edward or at least start shouting at him. Maybe now was a good time to intervene, she walked into the tea room and looked at Edward.

"I was just about to dish up supper," she said. "Would you like to stay?"

"Edward has a long journey back," Jessica answered, "and the M4 can be a nightmare in the evening."

"A spot of food will do you good then," Ellie said.

Jessica looked at Edward. "You didn't need to drive

down here, you could have just telephoned me," she said. Her voice had lost some of its edge.

"I tried but you didn't answer, and I just wanted to make sure you were alright, your text said you'd come here and you didn't know how long you'd be staying," Edward said. "I thought something terrible had happened. How long are you staying?"

"Not sure, I've booked a week off work," Jessica answered.

"That'll give me time to finish the nursery," Edward said smiling.

"You don't need to finish the nursery, there's plenty of time to do that," Jessica said, her voice rising again.

"I know but we want to be ready," Edward said. "The next few months will fly by."

"Look just go back home," Jessica said.

Edward looked hurt. "I know you're tired at the moment but I am trying you know. This is all new to me as well," he said.

"Maybe, but it's not going to change your life is it?" Jessica said.

"Of course it is, and I'm glad." Edward said. "I can't wait for the days out at football matches or ballet classes and, of course, another brother or sister."

"Stop, okay, just stop. I'm going to bed, I'm too tired for this right now," Jessica said. She walked out of the tea room into the hall.

Edward looked at Ellie. "I guess she's not feeling great right now but I don't know what else to do," he said.

Ellie noticed his eyes were brimming with tears. "I don't know what's wrong but I'll try and have a talk with her," Ellie said. "Do you want something to eat before you go?"

"No thanks, I'd better get back else I'll only make things worse," Edward replied.

"Well drive safely and stay in touch," Ellie said. She

put her hand on Edward's shoulder. "I'm sure it'll be fine. She just needs some time."

After Edward had gone Jessica came back into the tea room and sat at one of the tables. She pulled a corner of the tablecloth into her hand and started to twist it.

"What was that all about?" Ellie asked. "It did seem like you were being a little unfair, unless there's something you're not telling me."

"You wouldn't understand," Jessica said.

"Try me," Ellie said trying to keep her voice as gentle as she could.

"I'm tired Mum. Can we talk about it tomorrow?" Jessica said. She dropped the corner of the tablecloth and stood up. "I really am going to bed now."

5

Michael knocked on the door at nine-thirty. Ellie made a pot of tea and laid a tray for two. This tea was grown in Cornwall, she'd only discovered it recently and it had quickly become a bestseller.

"Here's a sample of the cake," she said. She gave him a lilac and pink coloured cupcake covered in green icing with little silver stars on top.

Michael bit into it. "Mmm, this is delicious," he said. "Grace will love it."

"I've had some thoughts about the cake," Ellie said. "What do you think about a woodland scene with fairies having a party around a fire? I could include a tree trunk with a hollow, some little strings of lights and some logs for the fairies to sit on."

"That sounds fantastic," he said. "Is that possible by the weekend?"

"I'll do my best, one way or another you'll have a cake by Saturday morning," Ellie replied. "Can I ask about Grace, is she your daughter?"

"No, she's my niece," he replied, "I told my sister I'd organise this party, she's got enough to deal with at the moment and, to be honest, I wanted to do something to help. I've felt a bit useless during the past few months."

Ellie watched as Michael looked down at his teacup, she could see the look of concern and worry in the lines on his face. She didn't want to pry any further, Michael would tell her more if he wanted to.

"Ring me on Saturday morning before you come to collect," Ellie said. She handed him a business card.

"Will do," he said as he got up to leave. "And thank you, you're going to make a little girl very happy."

Ellie turned to clear the table and heard the bell jingle as Michael left.

"Hi Mum," a voice said.

"Marie," Ellie said with surprise. "I don't see either of you for months and then you both visit out of the blue."

"What do you mean?" Marie said looking a little confused. "I had this sudden urge to come and visit. I've just finished a contract and had a little time to kill so I jumped in the car and here I am."

"Jessica's here," Ellie said.

"Is she alright?" Marie said sounding concerned.

"She's fine, well maybe not totally fine. I'll let her explain," Ellie said realising she still didn't have a clue what was wrong with Jessica.

"Sounds like we're the proverbial bad pennies," Marie said laughing.

"No, I'm just surprised to see you both, a nice surprise though," Ellie said as she cleared away the tea tray.

"Mum, is it okay if I stay a few days? Like I said I'm between contracts so it seemed like a good time to take a break," Marie said heading towards the hall door.

"You, take a break, that's a novelty. I'm not sure you've stopped since uni," Ellie said.

"I know, I know. But with Jessica getting married and having a baby I've just been thinking that maybe I need to stay in touch a bit more," Marie said.

"Before you go up I've got something to tell you." Jessica said.

"Sounds ominous," said Marie. "Do you have a new man in your life?" she asked laughing as she pushed open the door to the hall.

"No, I'm selling the tea room," Ellie replied quietly.

"Selling or thinking of selling?" Marie asked letting go of the door.

"Selling. The photographer came round yesterday and the brochure will be ready any day soon so keep your room tidy in case I get any viewings," Ellie said.

"But Mum, are you sure you've thought this through,

this place is you, you can't give it to someone else," Marie said looking directly at her mother.

"I'm not giving it to anyone, I'm selling it. And maybe it was me but things change," Ellie said.

"What could possibly change?" Marie asked.

"You may not have noticed but I've been living here on my own for most of the last five years, so now is a good time to do something else," Ellie said. She really didn't think her daughters would be that bothered about the sale.

"Marie," Jessica screeched as she walked into the tea room. "What are you doing here?"

"I could ask the same of you," Marie said.

"Are you staying?" Jessica asked.

"Yes, for a while," Marie replied.

"Great, I need someone to have some fun with, it'll be just like old times," Jessica said hugging her sister.

Ellie looked at them both and smiled. "I'll make a pot of tea," she said.

6

Ellie didn't see much of the girls for the rest of the day, she was busy in the tea room and they were upstairs catching up. They did pop down once to see what sandwiches and cakes they could take for their lunch – at least some things never changed.

When the last customer had left Ellie turned over the closed sign, at last she had some time to catch up with her twins, she still had no idea why either of them had turned up out of the blue. She was always really pleased to see them but this was uncharacteristic, usually they planned their visits weeks ahead and rarely stopped overnight.

As Ellie straightened the chairs Jessica poked her head around the door.

"Bye Mum, we're off, there's a band playing locally so we're meeting up with some old friends. Don't worry about tea, we're eating out," said Jessica.

"Oh, okay," Ellie said. "I was hoping we could have a chat."

"We can," said Jessica as she walked into the tea room and gave her mother a hug. "Tomorrow."

Marie followed behind her. "We haven't had time together in ages, we'd almost forgotten how much fun we used to have," Marie said. "You don't mind do you?"

They weren't identical, in looks anyway, but sometimes they seemed so alike. They now led very different lives – Marie had her career and Jessica was married and expecting a baby. And yet when they were together they seemed more than similar - laughing at the same jokes, having the same opinion, even enjoying the same music. They definitely had a connection beyond being sisters. They always seemed to know when the other needed support, like today when Marie turned up shortly after Jessica.

"Of course not," Ellie said smiling. "You two enjoy yourself, perhaps we can have breakfast together tomorrow."

"That would be great," Jessica said. "We'll even cook so you can have a lie in."

"Well that'll be a first, have a great time," Ellie said as she watched them leave.

At least she'd have some time to get on with the cake this evening. A quick shower and something to eat and then she'd start work. She went upstairs and into the sitting room. She sighed. Make-up, a hairdryer, a mirror and various brushes were strewn across the coffee table. Ellie picked everything up and carried it all into the girls' bedrooms. Brings back memories, she thought. Jessica's bedroom was a real mess, clothes were strewn across the bed, floor, chair, everywhere except in the wardrobe. Even when she lived at home she generally wasn't this untidy, she hadn't even made her bed. Marie's bedroom wasn't much better, the only reason the bed was made was because she hadn't slept in in yet. Ellie shut the bedroom doors, at least there were no viewings tomorrow.

After she had eaten the remainder of last night's casserole Ellie went back down to the kitchen and took the cakes off the shelf. When she had baked them she didn't have a clear idea of what she was going to create, now she realised she would need both of the two smaller cakes to make her tree trunk. She placed one small cake on top of the other and then placed these on top of the larger square cake. The tree trunk was much too big, she'd have quite a lot of trimming and shaping to do. Ellie took great care in cutting the cakes to size and then removing a considerable amount from the centre to create the hollow. She put them back on the large cake, much better, now there was plenty of room to build up a scene. It would all be iced and decorated but she needed to get the structure right first. She looked at the offcuts of cake. Enough to create two logs for the fairies to sit on. She put the remainder in a tub — just in case. Tomorrow she could start icing and creating the flowers, toadstools and some small woodland animals.

Once she had finished with the cake Ellie flicked through her catalogue of decorations. She found some traditional looking fairies, quite grown up ones, and turned on her iPad to order them, she selected next day delivery but assumed they'd actually arrive the day after. Next, she browsed her favourite website of dolls house furniture and accessories and found some battery operated miniature strings of lights and a wood effect fire she could use as the basis for a camp fire. She particularly liked this site as she often found really nice miniature items she could use on her cakes. As always she'd give advice on the items used to ensure everyone knew they were not edible and not toys.

It was after eleven when she finished. She was making a mug of hot chocolate when she heard the girls come back.

"Did you have a good time?" Ellie asked. Not that she needed to ask judging by the noise they made as they came up the stairs.

"Yes, it was great, it's good to be back," Jessica said.

"I'd forgotten how much I love this place," Marie said.

"Well I remember a time when you both couldn't wait to get away, what was it you used to say — you wanted the big city, lots of lights and plenty of parties," Ellie said.

She remembered when they had first gone away to university, Jessica to Bristol and Marie to Manchester. It was at Bristol that Jessica had met Edward, when they'd graduated they'd both got jobs in the city, bought a house, got married, very much a fairy tale wedding, and were now having their first baby.

Marie, on the other hand, had been totally focussed on having a career. She'd had the occasional boyfriend but nothing serious. She'd moved to London and worked for one of the big advertising agencies, she'd worked day and night to ensure she got the promotions she wanted. She'd managed to buy a small apartment fairly close to the centre, no mean feat on her own and with London prices. She was living her life exactly as she'd planned it.

Neither Jessica nor Marie had shown any interest in staying in the small Cotswold town, in fact they'd probably used the word boring on more than one occasion.

"Yeah we know, but that was when we were younger," Marie said looking at Jessica.

"It wasn't that many years ago," Ellie said, "you're not exactly elderly."

"Maybe we've just got it out of our system," Jessica said. She looked at Marie and winked.

"Maybe. Well I don't know about you two but I've got to get up tomorrow so I'm off to bed," Ellie said yawning.

As she wandered into her bedroom she could hear her daughters talking about their evening and the friends they'd met up with. It sounded like they'd had a really good time and were enjoying being back here. Perhaps they'd visit more often when she moved.

7

The next morning Ellie woke up to the sound of her alarm. Alarm was a good word as she never slept this late, she only ever set it as a bit of security, just in case. Well this was one of those just in case mornings – she desperately wanted to crawl under her duvet and go back to sleep but instead she got up and headed for the bathroom. There was no smell of cooking bacon or fresh coffee so she guessed there wasn't the promised cooked breakfast waiting for her. As she passed the girls' bedrooms she could see they were not getting up anytime soon, that early morning chat would have to wait.

Half an hour later she opened the tea room door to let Pat in.

"Late night?" Pat enquired.

"Getting this cake done," Ellie said struggling to suppress a yawn.

"You really should stick to your guns and say no to these short notice ones, people should plan ahead," Pat said.

"I know, but this is different," Ellie said. "Somehow it really did seem important."

"I thought you'd have help this morning, what with having the girls back," Pat said as she put on her apron.

"I was hoping that too but they did have a late night, flat out both of them," Ellie said indicating upstairs.

"Well we'd better get a move on if we're going to open on time," Pat said as she headed for the kitchen.

Ellie rushed around changing tablecloths, checking salt and pepper pots and filling the sugar bowls with the little brown and white cubes she liked use. The water hadn't heated by the time the first customer arrived, if they wanted tea she'd have to boil the kettle.

By lunchtime the place was full and people were

waiting for tables. When this happened she operated a simple number system, she gave the waiting customer a numbered ticket and then called the numbers as a table became clear, it seemed more civilised than having people dash towards a table as soon as someone looked like they were reaching for their coat.

As she grabbed a tray of tea and spoke to a customer wanting to pay Jessica and Marie pop their heads through the door.

"We're off now," Jessica said. "We're going into Bath to do a spot of shopping, it's great being able to spend so much time together."

Ellie took a deep breath and smiled at them. "Have a nice time," she said. They didn't even seem to notice that she was run off her feet and could do with a little help. She thought it was great they were enjoying themselves and this probably seemed like a bit of a holiday for them but she couldn't help but worry about what their next move might be.

8

Once they had closed the tea room Ellie decided to grab a few sandwiches and get on with the cake. She mixed up a big batch of icing and divided it into smaller bowls to add colouring. A mid-green for the forest floor, brown might have been more realistic but with the tree trunk being brown she wanted some contrast. A dark brown for the tree trunk and logs and a dark green to create the effect of moss. She used a little icing to fix the layers of cake in place and then covered it all with the different coloured icing. Ellie used a knife to create a rough texture for the forest floor and a bark effect on the trunk. She decorated the two logs on a board and then carefully placed them on the cake. Finally, she added touches of dark green. Already the cake was starting to come alive. She covered it and placed it back on the shelf. One more night to complete it, there was still a lot to do but at least it was now looking achievable.

The girls hadn't yet arrived home from their shopping trip, Ellie decided to send them a text to let them know she was having an early night and would catch up with them in the morning. With that she turned off the lights and headed upstairs.

9

Ellie woke to the sun streaming through the window, this weather really was fantastic for the time of year and it was certainly bringing in plenty of customers, the seasonal staff weren't starting till next week but she was going to need some help today. She put the kettle on, went back into the hall and called Marie and Jessica.

"Come on you two, you can help me today, I'm expecting to be busy," Ellie said as she opened their bedroom doors.

There was no sound from Marie however Jessica mumbled, "okay, we'll pop down when we're up and dressed." With that she pulled the duvet over her head.

"No, you'll get up now and be downstairs before opening," Ellie said.

She went into Marie's room and opened the curtains.

"Oh Mum," said Marie covering her eyes. "I need more sleep."

"So do I but we've got a tea room to open so get up and be downstairs in half an hour," Ellie said.

"I can't be ready in that time," Marie protested.

"Yes, you can. Just get showered and tie your hair back. You can have a coffee and something to eat downstairs," Ellie said. "And make your beds," she shouted to them both as she went back into the kitchen.

Ellie made herself a coffee, went downstairs and started to prepare for opening. She did her usual round of putting on new cloths and turning on the hot water. Forty minutes later the twins walked into the tea room.

"It's not even opening time yet, surely we could have had an extra hour in bed," Marie said yawning. "What do you want us to do? We thought Jessica could greet and seat and I could take orders."

"Firstly, we need to get ready for opening, so could

you both refill all the salt and pepper pots and check the cutlery. I'll do the flowers." Ellie said.

"Don't you do all this the night before?" Jessica asked clearly surprised that they had to do anything more than unlock the door and display the open sign.

"I clean up the night before, that takes long enough," Ellie said. "Everything else is done in the morning. And secondly once the customers arrive could one of you clear the tables as people leave and the other do the washing up."

"Don't you have staff to wash up?" Marie asked.

"There's just the two of us this time of year and Pat needs to do the food whilst I take orders and prepare the bills. We share making teas and coffees. If we get a quiet time you're welcome to learn the ropes. And Jessica make sure you take breaks and sit down when you need to but tell me or Pat," Ellie said. The girls had been away for some time but she had expected they might remember a little of how much work went into running the tea room.

"Okay, Mum," Marie said. "Come on Jessica, let's get started."

"I've got a viewing booked in today so I'll need to leave you to it for a while, Pat will be in charge whilst I'm out," Ellie said looking away but not fast enough to miss seeing their look of disapproval.

Ellie watched them fill the salt and pepper pots whilst she put fresh flowers into the vases. She could hear them mumbling to each other and caught the odd word – something about this being some holiday. As Ellie put the last vase on the table Pat arrived.

"Morning girls," Pat said looking at Ellie with surprise.

"Morning," both girls replied with little enthusiasm in their voices.

"They're helping all day," Ellie said to Pat.

With that the first customer arrived. Ellie took their order and made up a pot of tea whilst Pat made up the sandwiches. A few moments later six people walked in.

"Jessica could you let Pat know we have a large table and then stay in the kitchen to tidy and wash up," Ellie said. "And Marie could you be ready to carry the teas and cakes to the tables."

"How come Marie gets the best job," Jessica said pulling a face.

"You can swap over in an hour," Ellie said, this seemed very much like working with a couple of teenagers except the teenagers she usually worked with didn't act like spoilt kids.

By midday the tea room was buzzing with most of the tables taken and a couple waiting to be seated.

"Come on Marie," Ellie said. "You need to get these tables cleared, we've people waiting."

"I'm doing the best I can," Marie said. "When's lunch break?"

"This is a tea room, you get a lunch break after lunch," Ellie said.

"This is slave labour," Marie said.

"This is reality, if you need a drink or are hungry ask Jessica to come out here so you can take ten minutes in the backroom. Only ten minutes though as we're about to hit our busy time," Ellie said.

"Busy time, how much busier can it get?" Marie said as she cleared another table.

****

At two o'clock the first potential buyers arrived to view the tea room, the estate agent had already told her the young couple were looking to move into the area and were particularly looking for a business to run together.

"Come on in, I'm Ellie," Ellie said. "Have you come far?"

"Not too far, Gloucester," the lady said. "I'm Sam and this is Chris." She held out her hand.

"I'll give you the tour, please ask me anything as we go," Ellie said leading the way to the kitchen.

"What's happened here?" Ellie said as she looked around the kitchen to see most surfaces covered with dirty dishes. "And where's Jessica?"

"Sorry," said Pat looking embarrassed, "Jessica went for a break a while ago, I'll go and find her when I've finished this order."

Ellie felt a flush on cheeks, her kitchen never looked like this, even when they were busy.

Ellie looked at the young couple. "We've had a surge of customers the last few days, the weather's brought them out I think, unfortunately the seasonal staff don't start until next week and it appears the unpaid help has gone AWOL," she said.

Sam and Chris both laughed, they didn't seem to be put off by the kitchen, and hopefully they could see beyond the dirty dishes.

Ellie took the couple upstairs, luckily the girls had left it reasonably tidy.

"These are my daughters' rooms," she said as she opened both doors. "I would say typical teenagers but they're a bit older than that."

At least the beds were made, not exactly the clean and tidy look she'd hoped for but they looked lived in rather than a total mess.

"This is just the kind of place we're looking for. We've seen a few places and some just looked staged," Chris said, "almost as if no-one really lives there."

Ellie smiled. "I know what you mean," she said.

"If it's okay we'd like to come back with my parents," Sam said. "They're helping us buy a place so we'd like their opinion."

"Of course," Ellie said. "Come on downstairs and I'll make you a pot of tea."

When they went back into the tea room things seemed

a bit calmer, there were still a lot of customers however the empty tables were cleared and no one seemed to be waiting. She'd make up a proper afternoon tea for Sam and Chris, that should give them a chance to get a feel for the place and hopefully give her a chance to show them that they didn't live and work in permanent chaos.

10

"Tea's ready," Ellie called out to her daughters.

Jessica and Marie walked into the kitchen as Ellie took the macaroni cheese out of the oven and placed it on the kitchen table alongside a bowl of salad tossed in her homemade dressing.

Ellie smiled. "This used to be the one time of day we could always spend together," she said.

"I did enjoy just sitting here and chatting," Jessica said.

"Are you going out tonight?" Ellie asked her daughters.

"No," they both said together. They looked at each other. "Too tired."

Marie looked at Ellie. "Look mum, we've been talking, we really don't think you should sell the tea room, we both love this place. We know you've worked hard and deserve to take more of a break so we thought I could do a business plan that will help you improve your profits, then you can hire more staff," Marie said looking quite serious.

Ellie took a deep breath. "As thoughtful as that is it is time for a change. If I kept the place on I wouldn't be able to let go. You know I've loved this place but I'm ready for something new. Let me show you the cottage, I've got the details here," she said.

Ellie took the brochure from the kitchen drawer, she smiled as she looked at the photograph on the front.

"Take a look," she said handing the details to Marie, "there are some lovely photos of the place, I'm sure you can see why I fell in love with it."

Marie glanced at the photo on the front and handed the details to Jessica. "Mum, this place is tiny, where are we going to stay?" she asked.

"It's got a spare room, and I can put a sofa bed in the sitting room if you are both down together. There's also an attic room, I'd need to do it up but that would be an extra room," Ellie said smiling at Jessica, "for the grandchildren."

"Don't you think you're being a little selfish selling the family home without talking to us first?" Marie said. "We could help you find a more suitable house."

"I think it's time to be a little selfish," said Ellie.

"I know," Jessica said with enthusiasm. "I could come back and help you."

"But what about Edward?" Ellie asked.

"I don't know, I'm not sure I want to go back," Jessica said quietly.

"Now you of all people should know how hard it is to bring up a child on your own," Ellie said.

"But I wouldn't be on my own," Jessica said looking down. "I'd have you."

"You know you're always welcome here but you also know how much a father is needed," Ellie said.

"I wished I'd known Dad," Jessica said with tears in her eyes. "I can't even say I have any memories. There's the odd time when something pops into my head and there's definitely a man in the picture but I can't see him, no details, not even the colour of his hair."

"You've got the photos," Ellie said.

"But I can't superimpose them onto my memories," Jessica said. The tears had started to fall down her cheeks.

"You were very young, only two when he died." Ellie said. She looked at her daughters and smiled. "Do you know he was over the moon when I was pregnant, when I told him we were having twins I remember him saying, 'excellent, two for the price of one.' When you were born he absolutely adored you both, I think he was secretly pleased you had different coloured hair though, he was really worried he wouldn't be able to tell you apart."

Jessica looked up. "Tell me more about him," she said.

"He would get up in the night if you cried and sing you back to sleep. Sometimes he'd get up even if you were settled and look at you both with such pride. You were fourteen months old when we took you on your first holiday. He held you by the edge of the sea and dangled your feet in the water." Ellie said. "I remember, Jessica, how you insisted on walking and then screamed as a wave came and covered your knees. Your father scooped you up and told the wave off just to make you laugh. You copied him Marie, you pointed your finger at the sea and made a very cross face," Ellie said laughing. "He would have been so proud of you both, he would have loved your graduations, the wedding and now the birth of his first grandchild."

Marie smiled at her mother. She had her eyes half closed as if trying to recreate the scenes in her mind. "So why didn't you marry again, or at least have someone else in your life? It's been a long time since Dad died, I'm sure he wouldn't have minded," she said.

"No, he wouldn't have minded," Ellie said. "For the first year or two I didn't really come to terms with the fact he wasn't coming back – ever." Ellie closed her eyes. "As you know I received a visit from two police officers and they told me there'd been an accident at his workplace, an explosion and fire. Three people died that day. Good job I had you both else I don't think I'd have got out of bed ever again. Having two year old twins was enough to fill more than the twenty-four hours I had each day. After the funeral and inquest I decided to move away and came here to Cirencester. At that point I had two demanding twins and a business to run so that didn't leave much time, or rather any time, for anything else. And I wouldn't have had it any other way." She opened her eyes and brushed away the tears that had started to form.

"So how come you're selling if you've invested so much into this place, if it means so much to you?" Jessica asked.

Ellie looked at her daughters and reached across to

touch their hands. "I guess I've finally reached a point where I don't need it anymore," she said softly.

Ellie picked up a spoon and served up tea.

"After we've eaten I have to finish the cake," she said. "Why don't you both get an early night? I could really do with your help tomorrow, after that perhaps we can have a day out together."

11

Ellie went back downstairs to the kitchen. She'd left the girls watching a film together, something they hadn't done since they'd finished university and gone their separate ways. She knew they stayed in touch and she often heard about the epic phone calls but there didn't seem to be much time for them to actually spend time relaxing together. Perhaps after these last few days they might try and meet up more often.

Ellie took the cake off the shelf, this was it, the last evening to turn the cake into something that would put a smile on Grace's face, and perhaps her mum's too. She took the battery operated fire, placed it on the cake and surrounded it with the logs she'd created. When she turned on the little light the fire looked quite realistic.

She pulled a stool up to the central table, sat down and began to mould toadstools and flowers. Once they were ready she painted them with food colouring. Ellie really enjoyed painting her creations rather than colouring the icing beforehand, the tiny variations meant that each decoration was unique. Whilst they dried Ellie placed the fairies on the cake and draped the strings of lights around the scene. Finally, she added the tiny flowers and toadstools.

Ellie looked at the scene and smiled, it really did look magical. As she stood up Jessica and Marie walked into the kitchen.

"We're sorry Mum," said Jessica, "for going on about you selling the tea room. It was just such a surprise."

Ellie walked across to her daughters and gave them both a hug. "I should have told you sooner, but I really didn't think you'd be that interested," she said.

"We'll help you finish up," said Marie, "it'll be just like the old times."

"Not the old times as I remember them," Ellie said laughing. "Perhaps we can start some new old times and you two can help with the washing up."

"I get to lick the spoon," said Jessica as she reached across the worktop to grab the bowl with the remains of the icing.

Marie laughed and also reached for the bowl.

Everything seemed to be in slow motion. The girls reached for the bowl, it slid across the table, knocked the cake stand and the cake slid off the table onto the floor. As it hit the floor it split and crumbled.

Ellie looked in disbelief, she couldn't speak, she felt hot tears trickle down her face. She had put her heart and soul into this cake, she'd wanted it to be as near perfect as possible, and now it was just a pile of crumbs. Ellie put her head in her hands and sobbed.

"Oh, Mum," said Marie. "We're so sorry."

Ellie looked up at the distraught look in their faces. This was just an accident after all, no-one had meant for this to happen but knowing this didn't help, she couldn't control her tears as they continued to drip onto the cake on the floor.

"Perhaps you could make another," said Jessica. "It would only take a couple of hours to put together a sponge and a bit of icing, I'm sure there are some candles around here somewhere.

Ellie looked at Jessica. "I don't want to put a bit of icing on a cake with a few candles," she said trying to keep her voice steady. "Not only do I never do that, this cake was meant to be special, for a little girl who's been through so much."

"Do you know her?" Marie asked.

"No, but I know about her and by making this cake I could have made a little difference to her life," Ellie said as she started to scoop up the cake from the floor.

Marie looked up. "It was an accident," she said.

"I know, I know," Ellie said softly.

Jessica walked over to the cupboard and took out the flour and sugar. "Come on," she said. "We can't put that one back together but we can make another." She sounded unusually assertive.

"He's collecting it in the morning," Ellie said.

"Well we'd better get a move on then," Jessica said taking the scales down from the shelf.

"Marie, you clean up the floor, we don't want any more mishaps, I'll turn on the ovens and Mum, you can do the magic by mixing it all together," Jessica said sounding quite bright.

"But," said Ellie.

"No buts, if we don't start we won't finish," said Jessica firmly.

Ellie looked at Jessica, she'd never looked so confident, so in control. Well she'd better do as she was told and start mixing.

Three hours later the cake was cooked, cooled, and cut ready to start the build. Ellie instructed Jessica and Marie on how to mix the icing and which colours to add. She started to build the tree with its hollow and cover the cake with green and brown icing. By one o'clock they had the basis of a woodland scene. Under Ellie's instruction they made branches, a log fire, toadstools, and tiny flowers. As she carefully placed each handmade object onto the scene the cake started to look magical. Together they added the fairies and little strings of battery operated lights that twinkled through the scene. At four o'clock the cake was finished. They carefully covered it and gave it a final look before turning out the kitchen lights.

Jessica laughed and turned to Marie. "When I said I fancied an all-nighter this wasn't what I had in mind," she said.

"Thank you," Ellie said hugging her two daughters.

"No Mum, thank you," said Jessica.

"Yes," said Marie. "Thank you, for everything. And even though I'll miss this place you're right, it is time for you to sell."

Ellie felt more tears run down her face. This time she let them fall.

12

Michael arrived at nine-thirty.

"Wow," he said when Ellie brought out the cake. "I can't believe you did this in less than a week, I have to admit that with the timescale I'd given you I was expecting a bit of icing and some candles."

Ellie laughed. "As if," she said.

"Grace will love it, I can't thank you enough," Michael said taking the cake box from her.

Ellie smiled and suppressed a yawn. "It was my pleasure, or should I say our pleasure," she said, thinking of the daughters she'd left in bed. "Give Grace my love and I hope she enjoys her party."

Michael paused. "Could I take you out for a drink, perhaps tomorrow lunchtime, as a way of saying thank-you," he said.

"You've already thanked me, and it really was a pleasure even if a little challenging," Ellie said.

"Please, I would very much like to," Michael said a little hesitantly.

Ellie looked at him, he did seem nice enough, she didn't know him at all but perhaps now was the time to take a small risk, meeting at a local pub couldn't hurt.

"Okay, I'd like that," she said.

"Shall I pick you up, I know a lovely place a few miles from here," he said smiling.

"I'd rather stay in town if that's alright, there's a great place just up the road. I've got my daughters visiting so I don't want to be away too long," Ellie said.

"Up the road it is then, if I don't have to drive I can join you with a drink," Michael said.

Michael picked up the cake and left just as Marie walked into the tea room wearing her dressing gown.

"I overheard that," Marie said grinning. "I know we

said you should meet someone but we didn't mean arrange a date with the first stranger you see."

"He's not a complete stranger," Ellie said. "Anyway I'm not sure I want to go out with any of the men I actually know especially as most of them are married."

"Shall we come with you just in case?" Marie said.

"I don't think so," Ellie said. "I'm a grown woman, I'll be fine."

Ellie smiled remembering the times she'd been tempted to follow her daughters on their dates – just in case. She didn't actually do it, instead she just stayed awake until they came home and then pretended she'd been asleep for ages. How times had changed, she certainly hadn't expected this role reversal.

13

Ellie turned the sign on the tea room door to open. Today was going to be another hot one which meant busy. As she walked back to the kitchen the bell jingled.

"Hi Ellie," Edward called. "Is it okay to come in?"

"Of course," Ellie said. "Jessica's upstairs." Whatever the problem was between Jessica and Edward she hoped they could work it out.

"If it's alright with Jessica could I stay?" Edward asked as he headed towards the hall door. "I'm not sure what her plans are but I'd like to spend some time with her."

"Sure," Ellie said. "It'd be good if you two can sort things out."

Edward looked at her. "I'm not sure there's much to sort out. She's been a bit tired and techy but hopefully the rest has done her good," he said.

"Edward, I do think you should talk to her, see what's on her mind," Ellie said. "I don't know what's wrong but clearly something's troubling her."

Edward had a look of concern on his face. "I'll do that," he said.

Ellie followed him up the stairs and into the kitchen, she needed a quick caffeine fix before starting work.

Surprisingly Marie and Jessica were already up and, even more surprisingly they were washing up their breakfast bowls.

"Hi Jessie," Edward said as he walked up behind Jessica and kissed her on the cheek. "Are you feeling any better?"

"I wasn't feeling bad to need to feel better," Jessica replied as she walked away and wiped the kitchen table.

Edward looked a little taken aback but continued. "I thought we might spend the day together doing something, what do you reckon?" he said.

"I've got plans today, I'm off out with Marie," Jessica said without looking at him.

"Oh," he said, he looked hurt.

"Jessica," Ellie said, "Edward's come all this way to see you, you can change your plans."

"But I haven't seen my sister in ages," Jessica protested.

"You've seen her all week. In any case I need Marie's help so you are free to go out," Ellie said.

"I thought I'd done my stint," Marie said.

"In this place there's a stint every day," Ellie said, "and if you're both here tomorrow could you cover lunchtime as I'm going out."

"I'm not heading back until Monday," Edward said. "I've booked a day off work. If you like I can help out too." He sounded quite enthusiastic.

"That would be great Edward, thank you," said Ellie.

Ellie made a cup of coffee and carried it back downstairs. She glanced around and realised she'd have to have a bit of a tidy up as the potential buyers were coming back for a second viewing next weekend. At least she'd have some extra staff next week.

As predicted the tea room was busy for most of the day. Marie proved a real asset and was soon taking orders, seating customers and even using the coffee machine.

"Thanks Marie," Ellie said as they closed up.

"I've actually really enjoyed it," Marie said. "I'm even looking forward to working here tomorrow."

"I'll miss you both when you're gone," Ellie said. "We must have a day out before you go back."

"How about tonight?" Marie said.

"I'd love to but I really need to get some sleep," Ellie said yawning. "I know it's early but I think I'll go straight to bed."

"You go on up and I'll clean up," said Marie. "You

deserve a rest."

Ellie hugged her daughter. "Thanks again," she said.

14

Ellie opened the tea room door, looked up at the blue sky, closed her eyes and felt the warmth of the sun on her face. This was the first Sunday of the Easter holidays. Families had arrived in town yesterday and today they would be making the most of this glorious weather. She set up the tables outside, even here she liked to put out small vases of fresh flowers.

Pat had arrived early and Edward was already helping her in the kitchen. The girls were nowhere to be seen; another late night last night, at least they'd taken Edward with them.

Ellie walked back into the kitchen and turned on the urn.

"Thanks for helping out," Ellie said to Edward. "It's going to get a bit hectic later on."

"I've always fancied being a chef," he said, "well maybe not a chef but at least doing something like this."

"Have you had much experience?" Pat asked.

"Well I have cooked the occasional Sunday roast and I do a mean boeuf bourguignon," he said laughing.

"Maybe we should start with a few sandwich fillings and move onto the French cuisine this afternoon," Pat said.

"Hopefully the girls will be down before the customers arrive," Ellie said. "I would like to get away early enough to get changed. I'll probably get asked for drinks if I go into the pub like this," she continued indicating her black clothes and white apron.

As if on cue Jessica and Marie walked into the kitchen.

"Dressed and ready for action," Marie said saluting Ellie.

15

At eleven o'clock Ellie went upstairs to get changed, the tea room was busy but everyone seemed to be coping well. She'd already spent some time earlier deciding what to wear, she didn't want to give the impression she'd tried too hard and yet she wanted to make sure she looked smart. She had decided on a pair of smart jeans, a fitted t-shirt and a lightweight tweed jacket, although she probably wouldn't need the jacket. She looked at herself in the mirror. It had been a while since she'd been out with a man, this wasn't exactly a date but she still felt nervous.

"Mum, Michael's here," Marie called up the stairs.

"On my way," she said smoothing down a stray strand of hair before heading downstairs.

"Hi," Ellie said to Michael as she went into the tea room.

"Hi," Michael replied. "Ready?"

"Ready," Ellie said.

Ellie looked at Pat. "You've got my number if you need me, I'll only be up the road," she said.

"Go and enjoy yourself," Pat said. "We'll be fine."

Marie leaned towards Ellie and whispered in her ear. "And you've got my number if you need me," she said.

"Very funny," Ellie said as she walked out of the door.

"Bye," said Jessica, popping her head out of the kitchen.

Ellie and Michael walked towards the pub.

"It's such a lovely day," said Ellie. "Why don't we grab a coffee from across the road and have a walk in the Abbey Grounds instead?"

"Sounds good to me," said Michael.

Michael ordered two lattes and selected two slices of cake. "I guess this is a bit of a busman's holiday for you," he said.

"Not at all, good cake is good cake," Ellie said smiling.

They took their coffee, walked around the side of the church and followed the path towards the Roman wall.

"How did the party go?" Ellie asked.

"Great. Grace was blown away by the cake, I think I've become her favourite uncle," Michael said laughing. "Of course, that's not difficult as I'm her only uncle. The party was a real surprise. Grace knew we were taking her out so she got dressed up. We drove her to the village hall, it's still a bit far for her to walk, and when she walked in everyone let off party poppers and started singing Happy Birthday."

"She must mean a lot to you," Ellie said.

"I don't have any children myself, never been married, so yes Grace means a lot to me as does her mum. We're twins you see and to see her struggling so much after the accident was really hard," Michael said looking at Ellie.

"I have twin daughters and I often see how connected they are so I get what you mean. You said they had an accident," Ellie said.

"Yes, quite a few months back. A car slid on some mud, back in the autumn, and ploughed right into them. Grace was on the passenger side and took the full brunt. There were a few days when we were told she might not make it. Laura, my sister, just sat by her side hour after hour even though she was told to rest because of her own injuries. She had Grace quite late in life, she'd struggled to conceive and eventually had IVF so, whilst I'm sure all children are special, to Laura Grace was a real gift," Michael said. He pulled a cotton handkerchief from his pocket and wiped his eyes.

"What about Grace's father?" Ellie asked.

"He's in the army, he was serving away at the time, he was able to get back but it took a few days," Michael said. "As you know she pulled through. But that was just the start. Her leg had been shattered, there was talk of removing it, but after several operations and a long stint in hospital she's on the mend. She'll have to have check-ups and x-rays to make sure everything's okay as she grows but things are looking good."

Ellie put a hand on his arm. "Well I think she's really lucky to have you as an uncle," she said.

"Well that's me, what about you? You say you have twins," Michael said.

"Yes, twin daughters, their father died when they were two so I moved here and opened the tea room. They're grown up now, both moved out even though they've both come back to visit this week. And now I've decided to sell up and do something different," Ellie said.

"I've only just met you and you're leaving," Michael said laughing.

"I'm not going far, just outside Cirencester." Ellie said.

"Can we do this again, soon?" Michael said.

"I'd like that," Ellie said. "Give me a ring."

Ellie finished her coffee and continued to walk around the grounds with Michael. When they reached the pond she threw a few crumbs to the ducks and thought briefly about her future. She was enjoying Michael's company but she wasn't sure if this was the right time to start a relationship, not that Michael had asked for one. Once the tea room was sold she wanted to spend more time with the girls and help Jessica with the baby, and then she wanted to travel. Although she was sure the occasional coffee wouldn't hurt.

"Penny for them," Michael said.

"Sorry, I was just thinking I need to get back to the tea room," Ellie said. "The girls seem to know what they're doing but I can't leave them for too long especially as this is a sort of holiday for them."

"Come on then," Michael said. "I won't persuade you to stay but only because I intend to repeat this in the very near future."

"I'm already looking forward to it," said Ellie.

****

Ellie said goodbye to Michael and walked back towards the tea room. She could see it was busy, all of the outside tables were taken. It would only take her ten minutes to dash upstairs, get changed and be ready to help out. Ellie decided to go in through the tea room door, at least she could assess the damage and work out where she was most needed.

The door was open, as she approached Marie came out carrying a tray of tea and cakes.

"Hi Mum," Marie said. "Did you have a good time? You haven't been gone that long."

"Hi," said Ellie surprised at how well organised everything seemed. "Yes, and no, I think. I decided to get back and give you a hand, I know how busy it gets."

"No need," said Marie as she put the tray on one of the tables. "All under control. Why don't you take the rest of the afternoon off."

"Thanks," Ellie said as she looked through the door and saw Jessica clearing a table ready for a waiting family. "But I'll still pop back down if that's alright."

16

Ellie liked to spend Sunday evenings making cakes and scones for the week ahead. Even though they baked every day she liked to start the week with plenty of stock. She'd left everyone upstairs watching TV, clearly exhausted from working in the tea room.

She sat on a stool with pencil in hand ready to write a list of the cakes she needed.

"Sorry Mum," said Jessica as she walked into the kitchen.

"For what, I thought we'd got over the moving thing," Ellie said.

"For just turning up and thinking you should always be there when I have a crisis," said Jessica.

"I will always be here," Ellie said smiling. "Are you having a crisis?"

"Maybe, I don't know," said Jessica sitting next to Ellie.

"What's really up, is it Edward?" said Ellie.

"Not really, he's just trying to make everything go well, take the pressure off me. The thing is I don't think I can cope. I really don't think I'm ready to have a baby," said Jessica.

Ellie looked at the tiny bump. "Whatever your doubts I don't think you have much choice," she said.

"Don't get me wrong I do want the baby but... what if I'm a terrible mother? What if I don't do as good a job as you? I'm not sure I have the faintest idea about what to do and, if I'm honest, I feel absolutely terrified," Jessica said twisting the edge of her shirt. "I don't know how you did it, two young children and a business, you seemed to manage with ease. Me, I can't even manage a day at work and summon up any energy to paint the nursery. I don't think I'm going to manage, especially when Edward has to go back to work. Can't I just come and live with you, you could help me, you know what to do."

"Oh Jessie, stop comparing yourself to others, least of all me," Ellie said. "You do realise it was all an illusion don't you? I didn't actually manage it that well at all, I just tried to get to the end of each day without any major disasters."

Jessica laughed, though she continued to twist the edge of her shirt. "But what if I'm a rubbish mum?" she said.

"You are going to be a great mum, trust me," Ellie said, putting her arm around her daughter. "Do you know when you were first born I looked at you both and worried how on earth I was going to look after the two of you. Life before you were born was so simple. I had a job but, as long as I did that, I could get up when I wanted, eat when I wanted and go to bed when I wanted. Then all of a sudden I had responsibilities. I couldn't lie in just because I felt like it, and I had to get to bed early just to make sure I had enough sleep to be able to get up at midnight, and four o'clock and six o'clock. But do you know what, I wouldn't have changed it for the world. Every time I looked at the two of you I felt like the luckiest person alive. Watching you both grow up just could not compare to what I thought I was giving up – the parties, late nights out with friends, Sunday mornings in bed - it was all fun but not a patch on the love I felt for you."

"But you seemed able to do everything," said Jessica.

"Seemed, maybe, but the reality was very different," Ellie said smiling at her daughter. "There were many days when I thought I was letting you both down and I often wondered why customers came back to the tea room considering how rough I felt. I certainly didn't look capable of making a cup of tea let alone run a tea room or bring up two children."

"I think you're exaggerating a bit Mum," said Jessica laughing. "All I can remember is you doing a great job. Lots of games, the occasional telling off for not doing our homework, and always being there when we needed you."

"And you'll do a great job," said Ellie. "If you have an off day, I'm not too far away. And you have Edward, don't cut him out, let him enjoy being a father. Your father, even if it was only for a brief period, took every opportunity to be with you. Allow Edward to share in the joys as well as the challenges."

Tears started to roll down Jessica's face.

Ellie held her tighter. "Look if it would help I could put off selling the tea room for a while," Ellie said.

"Maybe, no, I don't know, that wouldn't be fair," said Jessica wiping her eyes with a tissue. "It just seems that everything is changing so fast."

"I used to think that when you were growing up," Ellie said. "Remember, I'll only be a phone call away."

"Not if you go travelling," said Jessica, still sounding tearful even though she was smiling.

"I promise I won't go away, well not more than a few hours anyway, until you are settled with the baby, okay," said Ellie trying to reassure her daughter.

"Okay," said Jessica.

"Right, come on, help me get these scones made," said Ellie getting up.

"If it's alright with you I think I'll go and have that chat with Edward, maybe suggest we go and choose some paint for the nursery tomorrow," said Jessica.

Ellie smiled at her daughter. "I think that's a great idea," she said.

17

Ellie woke feeling refreshed; this weather showed no sign of breaking and the seasonal staff started today. Adam and Jo had worked for her before so they both knew what they were doing. Adam was at university and only worked during the holidays but Jo went to the local college and was happy to work weekends and the occasional weekday if it didn't clash with her lectures.

As she sat up she could hear voices downstairs, a bit early for Pat and she wasn't expecting the staff for another two hours. She threw some clothes on and went down to the tea room. Edward and Jessica were getting the place ready, they'd already changed the cloths and were filling the salt and pepper pots.

"Morning Mum," said Jessica

"I thought we had uninvited guests," said Ellie laughing.

"No, just thought we'd help out," said Jessica. "Well actually it was Edward who said we should help, he pointed out how busy you'd been."

Edward looked at Ellie. "Sorry if we worried you," he said.

"No, I could tell it was friendly voices," said Ellie.

"We're heading back in a couple of hours, so I thought I'd cook everyone breakfast before we go," Edward said. "We've already packed and we've left the room tidy ready for any viewings."

"Wow," said Ellie looking at Jessica. "Are you sure my daughter hasn't been abducted by aliens and replaced by an imposter?"

"Very funny Mum, I haven't been that bad, well maybe just a little, but...," Jessica said her words trailing off.

"I was only joking, you know it's always great to see

you, in fact I'm hoping to see a lot more of you both now," Ellie said. "Maybe I can come and stay with you for a few days and then I can leave towels on the floor."

They all laughed.

"I'll just pop up to the butchers," said Edward, "and pick up some bacon and sausages. Then I'll do that breakfast."

Edward cooked up a fantastic full English. Not only had he bought bacon and sausages he'd picked up some mushrooms, tomatoes and black pudding. The kitchen looked remarkably tidy considering he'd had every hot plate in use and several pans on the go.

Ellie looked at Jessica. "It's been wonderful seeing you even if we haven't had much chance to spend time together. But that is going to change," she said.

She then turned and looked at Marie. "If you're staying for a couple more days perhaps we could go out one evening," she said smiling.

"That would be great Mum," said Marie "I'm here until Wednesday then I have to get back, I've got some prep to do for next week."

Edward collected the suitcases and brought them into the tea room. "Ready?" he said looking at Jessica.

"Yes," said Jessica. "See you soon Mum, very soon."

"Don't worry," Ellie said putting her hand on Jessica's arm. "Even if it takes a few months to sell the tea room I'll make time to come to Bristol, if need be I'll get some extra help."

"What you, let someone else take control," said Jessica.

"I think that over this last week I've said goodbye and moved on just a little," Ellie said looking around the tea room. She stared at the photos, paintings and prints on the wall, all were of the local area and most were by local artists. In the early days she used to wander down to the market and buy the occasional picture, it had helped her build a connection with the area. Nowadays artists tended to come to her and ask if they could display their work, this worked well as it gave her a constant supply of new paintings. She'd probably select one or two paintings to take with her but most she'd leave behind.

Jessica gave Ellie a hug. "Thanks Mum, for everything," she said. "We'd better get going if we're going to do some shopping." She turned to Marie, "Thanks for a great week, we must get together more often, I've really enjoyed myself."

Edward picked up the cases. "Bye," he said following Jessica out of the door, "and I have to say I've had a good weekend too."

Ellie watched as they walked up the road and rounded the corner towards their car. Later today she'd definitely sort out staffing so she could spend more time with both of her daughters.

Ellie turned to Marie. "Would you like to see the cottage I'm buying? We could go after lunch," she said.

"I'd like that a lot," said Marie.

18

After lunch Ellie hung up her apron and went into the kitchen. "I'll be back before closing," Ellie said to Pat, "any major problems ring me and I'll come straight back."

"What exactly do you think could go wrong?" Pat said smiling. "We'll be fine,"

"I know but with this weather you might get a late rush," Ellie said.

"If we do we'll manage," said Pat.

Ellie drove the car off the driveway and made her way out of Cirencester.

Marie pointed out some daffodils that were in full bloom. "This area is beautiful in the spring," she said.

"It's beautiful any time of year," Ellie said. "I love this weather, but I think I like winter best, especially when it snows."

"Yes, and of course Christmas is wonderful - snow on the trees, clear nights with lots of stars, lights everywhere, the little Christmas market in Cirencester and the big one in Bath," said Marie.

"And don't forget the magical lights at the Arboretum," said Ellie.

"How could I?" said Marie. "The annual walk around the trees, hot chocolate and Christmas carols."

"We should go again this year, all of us," said Ellie. Ellie paused briefly. "Is something up Marie? It's unlike you to take time off work."

"I don't know," Marie said. "I love my job, but sometimes I feel a little isolated."

"What, in London?" Ellie said. London was the place Marie had longed to be even before she'd finished university. She'd said it was where it was all happening. Maybe it was just in her blood, her father had been born in London and saw no reason to live anywhere else.

"Yes, I've got friends," said Marie. "But when Jessica announced she was having a baby I felt a little detached from it all. I couldn't get to see her for three weeks. I think I felt a little homesick and perhaps more than a little envious that you and Jessica have your lives under control and... you seem close to each other."

"Oh Marie," said Ellie reaching out to her. "I'm close to both of you. And as for things being under control, well maybe we are just better at being swans, you know, serene on top but absolute chaos going on underneath."

Marie laughed.

"So what are you going to do?" Ellie said.

"Go back," Marie said. "I'm actually starting to miss my job, I was even working on my new project last night. I'm not sure about living in London though, maybe I need to move a bit further this way and commute. We'll see."

"When I'm glad you love your job, you've worked hard for it." Ellie said. "There was a time when I worried how you'd cope if you didn't get the job you wanted. Of course there was no need to worry, you were always going to be just fine."

"I am going to make time to come back a little more often though, if that's okay with you," Marie said.

"Of course it is, I'd be over the moon," Ellie said. "And I can come and see you more often once I've moved, there's some great deals on the trains and I can go direct from Kemble."

Ellie pulled into a carpark next to a village hall. "This is it," she said, "well the village anyway. Let's have a wander then I'll show you the house."

They walked past a small cluster of houses, a village shop with a Post Office, a pub and a church. They turned up a lane and Ellie stopped.

"This is it," Ellie said, pointing to a honey coloured stone cottage with a sold sign outside.

"Wow," said Marie. "I can see why you fell in love

with it. The garden is beautiful, you can see it'll be a riot of colour in the summer."

"And that's just the front, the back garden has a vegetable plot and a small orchard. Perhaps we can fix up a swing in one of the trees," Ellie said. "There's only two bedrooms so I'll have to sell some of the furniture but the kitchen is huge so I should be able to do some serious baking."

"Well I for one can't wait to visit," Marie said.

Ellie hugged her daughter. "I'm glad you like it," Ellie said smiling. "We ought to get back though, I want to see Adam and Jo before they leave today."

19

"Hi Pat," said Ellie as she walked back into the tea room. "How is everything?"

"Absolutely fine, the staff have been fantastic, really looking after our customers," Pat said smiling at Adam and Jo.

"Great, I'll help finish up," said Ellie.

"Before you do you've got visitors, they're in the back room," said Pat.

Ellie was puzzled, she wasn't expecting anyone and the estate agent hadn't booked in any more viewings. Marie followed her through the hallway.

"Jessica, Edward what are you doing back, is everything okay?" said Ellie.

"Yes, Mum, well sort of," said Jessica looking a little nervous. "We got back and we were going to go to the DIY store but, well, my heart just wasn't in it. I couldn't get enthusiastic about paint colours or furniture or anything."

"Oh, Jessica," said Ellie.

"No, it's alright, we went out to lunch instead and we talked, a lot," said Jessica twisting the strap of her handbag. "You know I've been feeling, well, quite nervous about having the baby and, when I actually stopped to listen, turns out Edward is quite jealous of me getting to look after him or her so we had a long talk and made some decisions."

"Let me guess," said Ellie smiling and feeling a little relieved. "You're going to go back to work and Edward's going to stay at home."

"Not exactly," said Jessica twisting the strap even tighter.

Ellie looked from Jessica to Edward, they both looked quite nervous.

After what seemed like an age but was more like a minute Edward spoke up. "We'd like to buy the tea room.

Obviously we've got to sell our house in Bristol and of course we'd need to secure the loan but if we can get it sorted we'd like to put in an offer," Edward said without pausing.

Marie clapped her hands. "That's a fantastic idea," she said, "it's not too far for me to drive and I'd get to see my nephew or niece as often as I like."

Ellie looked from Jessica to Edward. "Are you sure you know what you're letting yourself in for?" she asked.

"Probably not," said Jessica. "But what better place to bring up a baby," she looked at Edward, "or two. We'd get to share looking after our little one and you'd be close by, that's when you're not swanning off all over the world."

"Oh Jessica, Marie, you know I'll always be here for you, whatever happens," Ellie said laughing. "Even if I do have to Skype from some remote island."

Pat walked in with a tray of teacups and a pot of English Breakfast tea. Edward stood up and poured tea into each of the cups. As he handed them around Ellie noticed her mobile light up. The text message read *Are you free Thursday night? Michael.* Ellie smiled. She had said it was time for some changes. She looked down at her phone and replied - *Yes.*

Marie picked up her cup. "A toast," she said, "to the end of an era."

Ellie raised her cup. "And to new beginnings," she said.

"To new beginnings," they all replied.

The End

Other Books by Lily Wells

The Vintage Tea Room 2
room for a small one

Jessica is determined to put her stamp on the tea room by baking and offering a range of Artisan breads. She plans to launch the new menu before the arrival of her first baby – in less than one month.

Jessica and Edward have recently taken over the tea room. Jessica soon realises that the customers love everything her mum has created – they do not want change - however, she wants to add something of her own. She decides that, despite having limited experience of baking, she is going to make bread. When her initial attempts do not turn out well it looks like she may have to rethink her plans.

Even though Jessica has not yet prepared for the arrival of the baby she is convinced she still has plenty of time to get her new venture off the ground. Babies, however, have a habit of foiling even the best laid plans.

The second book in the Vintage Tea Room series is a story of a young woman's determination, with the help and support of her family, to make a success of her new business.

The Vintage Tea Room 3
changing times and new opportunities

Marie has a decision to make – take the job in Copenhagen and move away from her family or give up on her dream of being at the top of the advertising industry.

When Marie arrives back in Cirencester for her

mother's wedding she can't wait to share the news of her new job with her twin sister, Jessica. To Marie's surprise Jessica is less than enthusiastic and gives her reason to wonder if now is the right time for such a move.

Marie does not want to burden her mum with news of her job or the reason she is having second thoughts. She confides in Adam, the temporary chef at the tea room. Despite being unsympathetic he may have the solution to her problem.

The third book in the Vintage Tea Room series is a story of an ambitious young woman who wants to both progress in her career and remain close to her family.

A Cornish Retreat

Cornwall seemed the ideal place for Lucy to get away and plan her future. Her fiancé had left her, she'd moved back in with her parents and her job didn't offer much in the way of prospects. If she was going to get her life back on track she needed a plan, and that plan didn't include starting a new relationship – until she met Jake. He appeared to be everything Lucy wanted – but could she really trust him?

The Cornish Cookery School
The Grand Opening

Alice has been left the Old Rectory by her Aunt Ruth. She'd loved spending her childhood summers in the large old house with its woodland and a secret path to the beach. These were happy times and the place held many good memories. Now the house looked tired, the garden was overgrown and the path to the beach was almost impassable.

Her parents are determined she should sell the house and concentrate her energies on her job in London, a job that doesn't bring her any joy. Alice has other plans, she intends to keep the house but has no idea what to do with it.

A chance meeting with local handyman Seb gives her an idea – turn the Old Rectory into a cookery school. But first she has to convince Seb to help her and he is less that keen.

The Cornish Cookery School 2
The Autumn Fare

Alice has been running the cookery school for only a few weeks and already has bookings into the next year. Life seems pretty much perfect but not one to stop and enjoy the moment she is already thinking of new ways to promote and grow the business. One of her ideas is to organise an autumn food fare to give local people the opportunity to see what they offer.

Her relationship with Seb is starting to develop into something more than a business arrangement however her parents have other plans for her love life when they make a surprise visit and bring along an old flame. They expect her to drop everything and entertain Michael with the hope that they will rekindle their old feelings for each other.

Just as Alice thinks she's got everything under control an overnight storm threatens to ruin everything. Alice and Seb have only a few short hours to turn a mud bath of a lawn and a collapsed marquee into somewhere that showcases their cookery school and impresses her parents.

Christmas in Cornwall

Heather has planned the best Christmas ever. She is going to spend Christmas Day with Nick, they are going to commit to their relationship and, finally, she will be able to introduce him as her boyfriend.

One phone call from her sister and her plans are thrown into disarray when Heather has to hot foot it down to Cornwall to help Sarah look after the children. She loves spending time with her nephew and niece but is worried that Nick doesn't seem keen to answer her texts or phone calls. As long as she can get back home on Christmas Eve she should still be able to get her plans back on track.

Printed in Great Britain
by Amazon

42676333R00040